Ladybird  Readers

The Monster Next Door

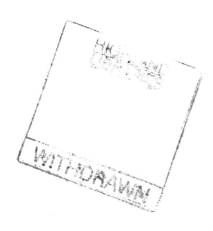

Series Editor: Sorrel Pitts
Text adapted by Sorrel Pitts
Illustrated by Gavin Scott

LADYBIRD BOOKS

UK | USA | Canada | Ireland | Australia
India | New Zealand | South Africa

Ladybird Books is part of the Penguin Random House group of companies
whose addresses can be found at global.penguinrandomhouse.com.
www.penguin.co.uk   www.puffin.co.uk   www.ladybird.com

First published 2016
003

Copyright © Ladybird Books Ltd, 2016

The moral rights of the author and illustrator have been asserted

Printed in China

A CIP catalogue record for this book is available from the British Library

ISBN: 978-0-241-25444-8

The Monster Next Door

Picture words

George

Green

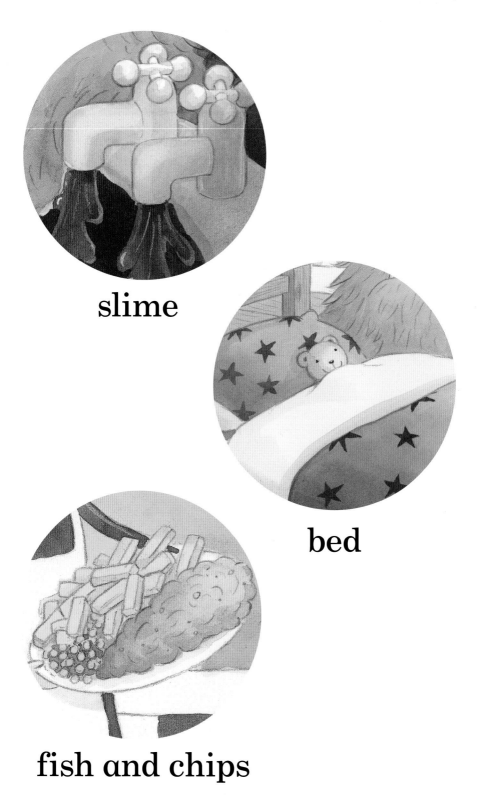

slime

bed

fish and chips

George was a normal boy,
with a normal family.

Green was a monster,
with a monster family.

George's house was next
to Green's house.

Green and his family lived in a monster house.

They took monster baths and ate monster dinners.

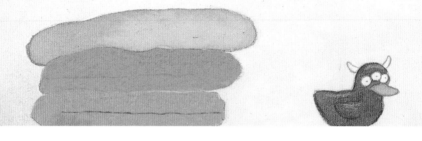

George and his family lived
in a normal house.

They took normal baths
and ate normal dinners.

Green played
monster games.

"I want to play monster
games," said George.

George played
normal games.

"I want to play normal
games," said Green.

"I want to be a monster," said George.

"I want to be a normal boy," said Green.

The next day, George went to Green's house. And Green went to George's house.

"Hello, Green!" said
George's mom. "Come in!
Your dinner is on the table."

"Hello, George!" said
Green's dad. "Come in!
Your dinner is on the table."

"This is our favorite dinner," said Green's dad. "We love green slime."

"Green slime?" said George. "Oh no! I cannot eat that!"

"This is our favorite dinner," said George's mom. "We love fish and chips."

"Fish and chips?" said Green. "Oh no! I cannot eat that!"

Green's dad took George
to the bathroom.

"Jump in the bath!" said
Green's dad.

"Oh no!" said George.
"I cannot do that. It's full
of purple slime!"

George's mom took Green
to the bathroom.

"Jump in the bath!" said
George's mom.

"Oh no!" said Green.
"I cannot do that. It's full
of water!"

George went to Green's bedroom. And Green went to George's bedroom.

"Oh no!" said George. "I do not want to sleep in a bed of purple slime!"

"Oh no!" said Green. "I do not want to sleep in a clean bed!"

Then, George ran back home and Green ran back home, too.

"I am happy because I am a monster," said Green.

"I am happy because I am a normal boy," said George.

Activities

The key below describes the skills practiced in each activity.

✏️ Spelling and writing

📖 Reading

💬 Speaking

❓ Critical thinking

✳️ Preparation for the Cambridge Young Learners Exams

1 **Look and read.**
Put a ✓ **or a** ✗ **in the box.**

1  This is Green.

2  This is a monster.

3  This is a normal family.

4  This is green slime.

5  This is fish and chips.

2 **Look and read. Choose the correct words and write them on the lines.** 📖 ✏️ ⬡

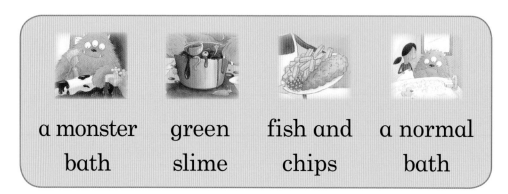

| a monster bath | green slime | fish and chips | a normal bath |

1 Monsters eat this.

green slime

2 This is a dinner for people.

....

3 People have this in their bathroom.

....

4 Monsters put purple slime in this.

....

3 Work with a friend.
Talk about the two pictures.
How are they different? 🗨

Example:

> In picture a, there are monsters in the kitchen.

> In picture b, there are normal people in the kitchen.

4 **Look at the letters.**
Write the words.

1 (m a l r o n)

George and his family are

n o r m a l .

2 (m e l s i)

Green's favorite dinner is

green ....

3 (n e r e g)

The monsters are ....

with big teeth and three eyes.

4 (h c p i s)

George's family love eating fish

and ....

5 **Look at the pictures.**
Tell the story to your teacher. 🗨

Example:

George lived next
door to Green . . .

35

6 **Read this. Choose a word from the box. Write the correct word next to numbers 1—4.**

| do | Jump | went | took |

Green's dad ¹ <u>took</u> George to the bathroom. "² _____ in the bath!" said Green's dad. "Oh no!" said George. "I cannot ³ _____ that. It's full of purple slime!" George's mom took Green to the bathroom, but Green did not want a bath of water. Then George ⁴ _____ to Green's bedroom.

7 Look at the pictures. One picture is different. How is it different? Tell your teacher. ○

1

In picture a, George is not there.

2

8 **Circle the correct word.**

1 Green enjoys monster baths in
   (**a** purple slime.)   **b** clean water.

2 Green enjoys eating
   a green slime.   **b** fish and chips.

3 Green's dad really likes eating
   green slime for
   a dinner.   **b** breakfast.

4 Green's family are not
   a monsters.   **b** people.

9 Ask and answer the questions with a friend.

1

> Do the monsters take a normal bath?

> No, they do not take a normal bath.

2 What is Green's mom doing?

3 Where is Green?

4 What is Green doing?

5 What is Green's dad doing?

10 **Read the questions and circle the best answer.** 📖 ✴

1 "Hello, Green. How are you today?"
   a "I'm very well, thank you."
   b "Goodbye."

2 "Can I go to Green's house?"
   a "Yes, you can."
   b "No, you do not."

3 "Would you like to play normal games?"
   a "Yes, please."
   b "Yes, there are."

4 "Do you like green slime?"
   a "Yes, I can."
   b "Yes, I do."

11 **Look and read.**
Put a or a X in the box.

1 Green's family are a
happy family.

2 Green's family wear
normal clothes.

3 Green has got two
eyes, a nose, and a mouth.

4 Green's family have got
normal hair.

5 Green thinks monster
games are fun.

12 **Complete the questions.**
Write *Who*, *What*, or *Where*.

1 ___Who___ has got a normal mom, dad, and baby brother?

2 _____ do Green's family live?

3 _____ sleeps in a clean bed?

4 _____ was in Green's bed?

5 _____ has got three eyes and very big teeth?

13 **Ask and answer the questions with a friend.** 🗨

1

> Which room is your monster room?

> My bedroom is my monster room.

2 What color is the slime in your room?

3 Can I come to your monster room?

4 Would you like Green's family to live next to you?

43

14 **Read the questions.**
Write answers using one,
two, three, or four words. 📖 ✏️

1 Did George want to go to Green's house?

Yes, he did.

2 Did Green want to go to George's house?

3 Did Green and George enjoy living in the house next door?

Do the crossword.

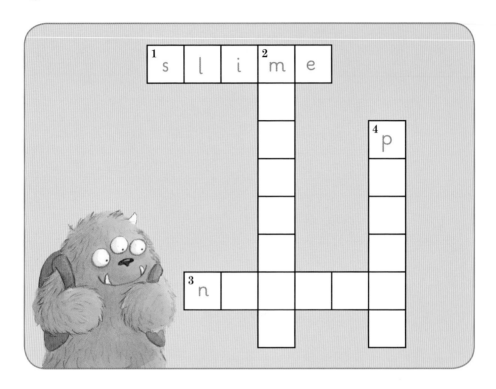

	¹s	l	i	²m	e

Across

1 Green's family love this!

3 Monsters are not this.

Down

2 Green and his family are not people, they are . . .

4 The color of the slime on Green's bed.

16 Write the correct words.

little brown long red pink short white

1 George's mom has got ___long___ ,

___brown___ hair.

2 George's mom wears a _____ ,

_____ dress.

3 George wears _____ ,

_____ trousers when he

plays football.

4 Green's mom wears a _____ ,

_____ flower in her hair.

17 **Look and read.**
Write yes or no.

George was a normal boy, with a normal family.

Green was a monster, with a monster family.

George's house was next to Green's house.

1 George and his family live next to Green and his family.   ....yes.......

2 Green is a monster with a monster family.

3 Green and his family are purple.

4 George lives with his family in a normal house.

Level 2

The Gingerbread Man

978–0–241–25442–4

Sly Fox and Red Hen

978–0–241–25443–1

The Monster Next Door

978–0–241–25444–8

Wild Animals

978–0–241–25445–5

Little Red Riding Hood

978–0–241–25446–2

Dinosaurs

978–0–241–25447–9

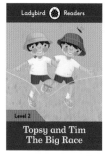

Topsy and Tim The Big Race

978–0–241–25448–6

Peter Rabbit Goes to the Treehouse

978–0–241–25449–3

Sports Day

978–0–241–26222–1

Going on a Picnic

978–0–241–26221–4

Now you're ready for Level 3!

Notes
CEFR levels are based on guidelines set out in the Council of Europe's European Framework. Cambridge Young Learners English (YLE) Exams give a reliable indication of a child's progression in learning English.